SPECIAL-EDITION
MOVIE NOVELIZATION

Published in the United States by Random House Children's Books, a division of
Random House LLC, 1745 Broadway, New York, NY 10019, and in Canada by
Random House of Canada Limited, Toronto, Penguin Random House
Companies. Random House and the colophon are registered trademarks of
Random House LLC.

randomhousekids.com

ISBN 978-0-553-51110-9

Printed in the United States of America
10 9 8 7 6 5 4 3 2

SPECIAL-EDITION MOVIE NOVELIZATION

Adapted by Victoria Shelley

RANDOM HOUSE 🏠 NEW YORK

CHAPTER 1

April O'Neil had always known she wanted to be a reporter. She had studied and worked for years and made it to New York City's Channel 6 News. But she wasn't happy.

April had just gotten a lead on the City's biggest story, the epic crime wave that had police paralyzed and citizens terrified. A dockworker she had interviewed revealed that the criminals had stolen a chemical used for genetic research. Was she following up that lead? Was she investigating the highly trained robbers called the Foot Clan, who were supposedly responsible? Was she reporting on their mysterious leader called Shredder, whom no one had seen?

No.

On the first day of spring, in the most exciting city in the world, April was in Madison Square Park, jumping up and down on a trampoline and flapping her arms like a bird. Her big story today was about a physical fitness trainer who had invented the Migration Diet.

"C'mon, everybody, flap your arms!" the trainer yelled as he bounced on a trampoline next to April. "No one's ever seen a fat bird, right? This is the best way to shed that winter weight."

It was absolutely humiliating. April knew that serious reporters didn't bounce. She didn't want to report live from a trampoline. She wanted to investigate the crime wave sweeping the City.

April knew she could find Shredder. She was the best investigator Channel 6 News had—only her colleagues didn't realize it. That was why her boss had given her the trampoline story. She had to prove herself.

April was frustrated. She wished she could talk to her dad about it. Sadly, he'd died years ago in a laboratory fire. These days the only one she could talk to was Vern Fenwick, her cameraman.

Once April finished her interview, she met Vern over by the news van where he was packing up his camera equipment.

"Four years of journalism school for this," April complained about the silly story.

"Look, O'Neil, I've worked with a lot of reporters like you," Vern said. "A lot of them went on to do big things. You know what they had in common?"

April shook her head.

"They *worked* for it. Nobody's going to just hand you a big story. You have to find one on your own and nurture it."

April looked at Vern. His wise words made perfect sense. *A good reporter nurtures a story,* she thought.

When they returned to the office, April went to work, checking and rechecking shipping records for the chemical the dockworker had mentioned. A little investigation led to a big discovery: another shipment of the chemical was expected that night.

April decided she would be there to meet it.

April biked across the dark Brooklyn waterfront. During the day, men unloaded huge containers from cargo ships, but at night there was no one around. She stashed her bike near an abandoned warehouse and walked toward a row of shipping containers. She looked carefully around the docks for clues. Maybe she would find evidence that would lead her to Shredder.

Suddenly, April heard tires squealing! She

looked up to see a caravan of trucks, vans, and SUVs screech to a stop. The doors of the vehicles flew open and armed men leaped out onto the docks. April ducked behind a Dumpster to hide, but not before she got a good look at the men. They were dressed like ninjas, and their faces were covered by Japanese theater masks. It was the Foot Clan!

The Foot Soldiers swarmed the shipping containers. They pulled cables, pulleys, and other equipment from their packs. They moved quickly and silently, attaching their cables to the cargo crates. They were going to steal them! April couldn't believe it. She was finally in the middle of the action!

April knew that a good reporter always takes pictures. She reached for her camera but never got the chance to use it. Three Foot Soldiers emerged from the shadows in front of her. They stalked toward her menacingly. Their eerie masks glinted in the moonlight as they drew closer. April had the feeling she was in serious trouble.

Just then, a cry went up along the docks. The Foot Soldiers were under attack at the shipping containers. They shouted and fired their weapons into the night. It looked like they were battling an unseen force. Someone or some*thing* knocked the soldiers aside and sent them flying across the docks. Some were dragged into the shadows. Others were whisked into the water as if by an invisible hand.

Even the soldiers surrounding April were plucked into the air and tossed into the Dumpster like yesterday's trash. It was so dark she couldn't see how it happened. She almost believed there *was* an invisible hand. But her reporter's instinct told her otherwise. She ran toward the shipping containers, determined to find out who or what was attacking the Foot.

Suddenly, there was a loud rumbling noise. One of the cargo crates appeared to be moving by itself. The giant metal box slid forward along the ground, gathering speed. The soldiers cried out in fear as the huge crate barreled toward them, knocking them all into the river.

Now alone on the docks, April hurried toward the crate. She was close enough to touch the container when it moved again. She took a step toward it and it lurched back an inch. Puzzled, she took another step. The crate inched away from her. April blinked in surprise. It was almost as if the crate was toying with her.

After a moment, April began to run. The cargo container scooted away from her. It slid all the way across the docks until it reached its original position. April knew there had to be someone moving the crate. She ran a complete circle around it, hoping to find out who it was. But there was no one there. All she found was a peculiar Japanese symbol spray-painted on one side. April reached for her camera and photographed the symbol.

CHAPTER 2

The Channel 6 newsroom was a busy place.
Reporters, editors, and producers hurried through
the tight maze of desks and cubicles. There was
no time to spare on the hunt for the next big story.

April was late. When she finally arrived in the
newsroom, the daily story meeting had already
started. Bernadette Thompson, the news editor,
looked up as April stumbled in. The rookie
reporter was carrying her laptop balanced on a tall
stack of papers.

"If it isn't the late-breaking April O'Neil,"

Bernadette joked. "It's your turn to pitch a story."

The other reporters and cameramen gathered for the meeting snickered. They didn't expect much from the rookie. Vern gave April an encouraging look.

April took a deep breath. This was the moment she'd been waiting for. She set her laptop down and handed out the papers she'd been carrying. "Last night, I witnessed at least two dozen Foot Soldiers attempting a major robbery at the Red Hook docks in Brooklyn."

"You're sure about this?" a reporter named McNaughton asked. "I didn't hear anything about it on the police scanner."

"Because someone stopped the attack," April replied smoothly.

"You're burying the lede, O'Neil! Who stopped it?" Bernadette asked, leaning forward in her chair.

"I know this is going to sound crazy, but I

think it was . . . a vigilante," April answered.

"A vigilante?" Bernadette said skeptically. "O'Neil, for you to propose such an unconventional theory, you'd better have some pretty definitive evidence."

April flipped through her papers and pointed to a picture of the Japanese symbol she'd seen last night. "I found this painted on a shipping container at the crime scene," she explained. "It's a Japanese symbol. It means 'family.'"

The veteran reporters chuckled, but April kept going. "The same symbol has appeared in other locations around the City. Japanese rulers used it to show that their soldiers would lay down their lives for one another . . . like a family. I think it's our hero's calling card."

Bernadette was unconvinced. "And other than this, you have . . . ?"

"Nothing," April admitted nervously.

Bernadette folded her arms across her chest. "I like you, O'Neil," the news editor said, "but these staff meetings are not a joke. If this happens again . . . well, let's just say there are a lot of girls out there who can do what you do."

April hung her head. She'd blown her chance at her first big story.

A *kunoichi,* a female ninja, knelt in a barren room lit by low, flickering candles. A dark figure emerged from the shadows. He was tall and draped in dark robes. His voice was a serpent's hiss.

"Karai, you failed me at the docks last night."

"I'm sorry, Master Shredder," Karai said, her head bowed. "It won't happen again."

"No, it won't." A long blade appeared from the folds of the master's robes. "These warriors that stopped you have a weakness. They seem to care for people. You must use this to set a trap for them. Destroy innocent people, if you must."

"Yes, Master."

Innocent lives did not matter to Karai, only the approval of her sensei. She was a fierce warrior, cold and calculating. Even members of the Foot Clan were wary of her cruelty and skill. It was rumored that she had a special connection to Shredder. Some whispered that she was his daughter, but no one could prove it.

That night April was stuck reporting another fluff story with Vern. This one was a fancy fund-raiser for a new community center. She had spent the past two hours interviewing guests about their fashion choices. She was more than ready to leave when Eric Sacks, the keynote speaker, stepped up to the podium on the stage.

Eric Sacks was a wealthy philanthropist who owned a number of important research companies. He was a major supporter of the community center.

"A long time ago, a close friend told me something I will never forget," Sacks said to the audience. "He told me that the greatest achievement for anyone is to simply be their best self."

April looked up. Those words were familiar.

"Since then, my philosophy has been to help people become the best they can be through companies like Sacks BioMed, Sacks Robotics, and Sacks Construction. This new community center is a step toward that."

April's eyes widened with recognition. This was the same Eric Sacks who had worked with her father years ago!

"So let us work together and take more steps like this," Sacks said. "And this seems like a fitting time to announce that Sacks Security has just struck a major deal with the City. We will now be in charge of the effort to battle the crime wave wrought by the masked gangs. With our technology and the support of the people, we will rid New York of crime and return it to its rightful place as the finest and safest city in the world."

The audience burst into applause. Sacks stepped down from the stage. April walked over to him and introduced herself.

"I can't believe it," he said. He hadn't seen April since her father's funeral.

"I just wanted to say that those words meant a lot to me," April told him. "I hope to live up to them someday."

Sacks smiled warmly at her. "It looks like you're doing a pretty good job. Channel 6—very impressive."

"Well, it's not exactly everything I dreamed

it'd be," she said sheepishly, thinking of the story meeting.

"April, as long as you are true to yourself, your father will always be proud," Sacks said. "Don't allow others to discourage you just because your path is different from what they want it to be."

He shook her hand and crossed to the exit, leaving April to dwell on his words.

CHAPTER 3

Later, April and Vern were driving back to Channel 6 in the news van. She was still thinking about what Sacks had said when she noticed a crowd charging down a side street.

April glanced over at Vern. He saw the look of excitement in her eyes.

"No, no, no, O'Neil. Don't even think about it," Vern said firmly. But before he had finished his sentence, April was out of the van and running toward the crowd. Vern sighed in frustration.

The frightened mob was coming out of

the subway. April weaved through the tide of people and raced down the stairs into the station. Everything was in confusion. Foot Soldiers swarmed the subway. April ducked back into the shadows to hide, but she wasn't quick enough. Several soldiers grabbed her from behind. They dragged her through the turnstiles onto the subway platform.

There, the Foot Clan was guarding a large group of hostages. April was brought to the front of the group. She had a clear view of the Foot's leader, a dark-haired woman. The woman was the only one of the Foot Soldiers without a mask.

"We know you're out there!" the woman shouted into the subway tunnels. "If you don't surrender, we'll start executing hostages!"

April wondered who the woman was talking to. The only people in the subway were Foot Soldiers and hostages. But then it dawned on her. The woman had to be talking to the vigilante, the superhero who'd stopped the robbery on the docks. This whole thing was a setup to get the hero to surrender.

April needed to take a picture. She slowly reached for her phone.

"Last chance!" the Foot's leader yelled. She raised her weapon and pointed it directly at April and the hostages. "THREE! TWO! ONE!"

April squeezed her eyes shut, expecting the worst. Loud music suddenly crackled over the subway's public announcement system. Something big was about to happen. She opened her eyes and readied her phone. The lights in the subway flickered on and off in time with the music. This was not at all what the Foot Soldiers had expected.

The music stopped and the subway went completely dark.

An express train roared through the station,

distracting the soldiers. They were so puzzled they didn't notice as two *sais* whistled past them. The twin blades spun through the air and pinned a Foot Soldier to the wall by his clothes.

The soldier screamed and the platform erupted into chaos. Like the night before, the Foot was under attack. Soldiers were tossed into the air and thrown the length of the platform. The dark-haired woman was pushed off balance, giving the hostages the chance to escape. April couldn't see who was helping them, but someone was there. It had to be the superhero!

Whoever this hero was, he had a sense of humor. He yanked down the pants of half the Foot Soldiers before they even realized it. He slammed their heads together like coconuts. He even rolled one of the soldiers like a bowling ball, knocking down the others like pins.

Within minutes the vigilante had tied up most

of the Foot Soldiers. The others, including the dark-haired woman, had escaped. As the hostages ran for the exit, April raced along the platform. She wanted to catch a glimpse of the hero. In the distance she spotted a dark figure slipping into an air vent. He was gone before she could raise her phone.

When she reached the vent, it was sealed shut from the inside. April couldn't get in, but she figured the vent had to lead somewhere. She ran back through the station and up to the street. Half a block from the station exit, she saw a ventilation shaft that ran right up the side of a tall building.

April noticed a rickety fire escape next to the shaft. She sprinted to the building and jumped to the rusty ladder. She climbed higher and higher, and at last she caught sight of the figure again. He was running along the edge of the roof.

"Wait! PLEASE!" April shouted.

The figure stopped at the sound of her voice. April kept climbing. She was only a few feet away from the vigilante. She was only a few feet away from the top of the roof and the biggest story of her life.

CHAPTER 4

A strong hand grabbed April by her wrist and pulled her to the rooftop.

It seems like the big story got me, she thought.

The vigilante stood in silhouette with the moon behind him. He stuck a heroic pose with his chest puffed out and his hands propped on his hips. April still couldn't see his features.

"Superman?" she asked hesitantly.

"Yep, that's me," a voice replied. "I look way different up close."

The vigilante stepped forward so April could

see him. She drew back in shock. Standing in front of her was the world's tallest turtle—only he wasn't exactly a turtle. He was human, too. Sort of. Instead of tall, dark, and handsome, he was tall, green, and muscular, with a round head and a shell on his back. He wore an orange bandana tied around his head with holes cut out for his eyes. A pair of *nunchucks* hung from a belt at his waist.

April started to scream.

"Chill!" the turtle said, holding up a hand. "It's just a mask."

April sighed with relief. So he *was* a masked vigilante. The turtle reached behind his head and untied his bandana. Now his entire turtle face was revealed. April's jaw dropped. She'd never seen a creature like this before. Her first instinct was to run.

She bolted in the opposite direction and ran straight into the muscular chest of another turtle creature! He looked just like the first turtle, only he wore a purple bandana. A long *bo* staff was strapped to his back. The turtle scanned her with a strange-looking device.

"I'm reading signs of hypotension and hypoperfusion," he said. "I'd say vasovagal syncope is imminent."

April screamed. She turned on her heel and stumbled into a third turtle—this one wearing a blue bandana. A *katana* sword was strapped to his waist. "Just take a deep breath, ma'am," he said patiently. "We're not here to hurt you."

April backed away from him, smashing into the last of the turtles. He stared angrily at her from behind his red bandana. Twin *sais* were tucked into his belt. He yanked the press badge from April's neck. It was the last thing she remembered before she passed out.

When April woke up, she was still on the roof. The four turtles were standing over her.

"Is she all right, Donnie?" Leonardo, the blue-masked turtled asked. He was the leader of the group, and he felt responsible for everyone's safety.

Donatello, the purple-masked turtle and the brainiest of the bunch, checked his instruments. "Vitals are within normal parameters," he replied.

"Great work, Mikey. Gold star," the red-masked turtle snapped sarcastically. His name was Raphael, and he wasn't happy about their guest.

"Leo, why are we even talking about this primate?" Raphael said harshly. "Mikey, toss her off the roof."

"No," Leonardo said firmly. "We're supposed to protect them. That's Master's first rule."

"Really?" Raphael asked, challenging him. "I thought the first rule was never to be seen." He swiped April's phone.

April charged at him, but two of the other turtles held her back. Raphael narrowed his eyes indignantly. He couldn't believe this woman would dare come after him. He took a threatening step toward her.

"Stand back, Raphael!" Leonardo said. The giant turtle stopped in his tracks. It was past time for the Turtles to leave.

Donatello grabbed the phone. With a few quick strokes, he learned April's name and erased all the pictures. "If she had pictures of us, they're gone now."

Leonardo looked directly at April. He gave her an intimidating stare. "Do not say a word about this to anyone," he said sternly. "If you do, we will find you."

The Turtles melted back into the shadows. She watched them run, bound, and jump across the distant rooftops. She managed to take one blurry picture.

April shook her head in wonder. She could barely believe what had just happened. The superhero that had saved the hostages was actually *four* superheroes. And those four superheroes were . . . turtles?

And their names were strangely familiar.

CHAPTER 5

"What do we tell the Big Cheese?" Michelangelo asked. He and his brothers were making their way through the sewers to their underground lair.

"The truth," Leonardo replied. "Why wouldn't we?"

"Spoken like a true Boy Scout," Raphael scoffed.

Leonardo stopped walking. "You think I asked to be the leader of this outfit, Raph?" he asked irritably. "You think I wanted this? Splinter chose me. I'm just doing my duty."

"Ha. Doodie," Michelangelo chuckled.

Everyone fell silent. The Turtles started walking again. Soon, they trudged into their lair. It was an abandoned sewer control room furnished with everything a teenage turtle could want. There were huge flat-screen TVs, computers, the latest video-game systems, and even a skateboard ramp.

The Turtles took off their weapons. They were tired after a long night of fighting crime.

"Maybe if we save enough people, if we do enough good, we'll be accepted up there," Michelangelo said, pointing toward the surface.

"Grow up, Mikey," Donatello said.

A large rat stepped out from the shadows. He wasn't just any rat. He was Splinter, the Turtles' teacher and master. Unlike most rats, he walked on two legs using a walking stick. Splinter was old and wise, with gray fur and beardlike whiskers.

"Where were you tonight, my sons?" Splinter asked.

"Oh, here and there," Michelangelo said. "Nowhere, really. Actually, I don't remember."

Leonardo could tell that Splinter was displeased. Maybe it wasn't a good idea to tell him about their adventure. He didn't say anything and neither did his brothers.

Splinter stroked his long whiskers. "Maybe some training will help you all remember."

The Turtles groaned.

The training was grueling. Each Turtle had to hold a difficult pose and meditate. Michelangelo did a handstand on one finger and balanced weights on his feet. Leonardo held a split between two chairs, eggs balanced on his hands and head. Sweat poured off Donatello's head. Raph's muscles ached.

But Splinter took the training to another level—with pizza!

He placed a box next to Michelangelo. The delicious smell of dough and cheese overpowered his nose.

"Many people know of the Three-Cheese Pizza," Splinter said. "But few are familiar with the Ninety-Nine Cheese Pizza!" He threw back the lid of the box, revealing the pie.

"I can't take it!" Michelangelo screamed as he crashed to the floor. "We went aboveground! We stopped a crime! We met a beautiful girl named April O'Neil! I need pizza!"

"We were seen," Leonardo confessed.

"Thanks to Mikey," Raphael muttered.

"Silence, Raphael!" Splinter said sternly. "You are brothers! You fight, you live, you die as brothers! If one of you was seen, all of you are responsible."

"She is a reporter, Sensei," Donatello said. "But I wiped her phone clean, so she didn't get a picture of us."

Splinter stared for a long moment. He

recognized this reporter's name. It brought back a memory from a long time ago. There'd been a laboratory . . . and a fire . . .

"April O'Neil," he said at last. He raised a hand to his forehead in amazement. "If she knows you are alive, she may soon be dead. You must save her life."

The Turtles looked at each other, confused.

"But, Sensei, why?" Leonardo asked.

"Because, my sons, she saved your life," Splinter replied.

"What are you talking about?" asked Raphael.

Splinter waved his question away. "All questions will be answered in time," the rodent said mysteriously. "Remember, my sons, this is a test of your brotherhood. If you have any hope of returning home safely, you must fight as brothers. As a family."

The Turtles turned to look at each other. They were completely bewildered, and all because of a reporter named April O'Neil.

CHAPTER 6

April burst into her apartment. She wanted to get to work, but her roommate, Taylor, was using her laptop. April pulled the computer away from the startled girl.

"Hey, I was updating my blog," Taylor protested.

April was already typing furiously and didn't hear her. "You'll never believe what I saw tonight. You know the vigilante story I've been investigating?"

Taylor nodded. April's story came out in

excited, fractured gasps—hostages, ninjas, heroes, a rooftop. Taylor couldn't follow. "So you met a super strong hero that fights crime? Are you telling me that your vigilante is really a caped superhero?"

"Aren't you listening?" April groaned. "I said *ninja,* not *superhero.* And they don't wear capes."

"They? There's more than one? Did you get their numbers? Are they cute?"

April shook her head. This was not helping, and there was no time to waste. She retreated to her room and slammed the door.

She spent the next hour researching information about turtles and ninjas and Japanese symbols. Finally, she went to an old box in her closet and dug out a videotape she hadn't watched in years. She slid it into a camera and pressed play. She saw herself on the monitor. She was eight years old.

"This is April O' Neil reporting live from my

dad's lab," the young girl said, staring into the lens of her handheld camera. "I know, it sounds super boring, but he actually does some pretty cool stuff. Follow me."

April remembered creeping through her dad's laboratory with her camera rolling. She knew she wasn't supposed to be there. Her dad, Dr. O'Neil, had been working on an experiment for Eric Sacks.

The video image showed rows of test tubes, beakers, whirring machines, and glass aquariums. The aquariums housed laboratory animals. April's favorite animals were four baby box turtles. Each of their shells was painted a different color: blue, orange, purple, and red. The turtles were playful and curious. Their names were Leonardo, Raphael, Donatello, and Michelangelo. They played, slept, and ate under the watchful eyes of a wise lab rat that lived in the cage next to them.

"Observe the bizarre eating habits of the box turtles in captivity," April said, filming the turtles. She picked up a slice of pizza from an almost empty box nearby and lowered it into the cage. The scent of pepperoni made the Turtles' eyes grow wide in excitement. They immediately crept over to the pizza and began eating hungrily.

April stopped the video. It was all so unbelievable, but it was also starting to make sense. She had wanted a big story, and now she had one. She emerged from her room, exhausted and exhilarated, and dropped onto the couch.

Taylor was in the kitchen, whispering into her phone. "I think she's really starting to lose it. Mom, I want to move back home."

Bernadette Thompson did not appreciate being called into the office at five a.m. April met

her at the door to the newsroom. She was obviously excited and speaking very quickly.

"Okay, so we've all heard stories about this superhero who's fighting back against the Foot Clan," April said. "I told you I saw him at the docks, but I didn't get a good look at him."

Bernadette heaved a frustrated sigh. "We went over this, O'Neil," she said. "There's not one shred of evidence that this guy's real."

"I saw him. Well, not just him. There were four of them," April said.

"Okay, O'Neil, I'll play along. What did the superheroes look like?" Bernadette asked sarcastically.

April told her boss exactly what she wanted to know. The superheroes were slimy and green.

"Green?" Bernadette asked incredulously.

"Most turtles are," April replied. "These are box turtles—*were* box turtles. Now they are all at least six feet tall! And they can talk!"

Bernadette was flabbergasted. She'd never heard anything so crazy!

April explained everything she'd learned the night before. She'd recognized the Japanese symbol—the one that meant "family"—from her father's lab all those years ago. She remembered that her father had been conducting experiments for Eric Sacks. She'd first met the box turtles in the lab. They were a part of the experiments. Somehow, the turtles had been mutated. April was sure of it.

"So let me get this straight," Bernadette said skeptically. "You're telling me that the vigilantes fighting Shredder and the Foot Clan are mutant ninja turtles?"

"Exactly!" April exclaimed happily. "I think they might be teenagers, too."

"I see," Bernadette nodded. "Mutant ninja

teenage turtles—when you put it that way, it makes total sense!"

"Really?"

Bernadette's response was brief: April was fired. She didn't even get a chance to show the blurry picture she'd taken of the escaping turtles.

Later, Vern offered to give April a ride home in the Channel 6 news van. It was the least he could do. But April had a better idea.

"I want to see Eric Sacks," she said. She had a hunch the wealthy businessman was at the center of this mystery.

"Oh no, O'Neil," Vern said, shaking his head. "You've got to put this to bed."

April glared at him. "All those great reporters you supposedly worked with . . . would they have put it to bed?" she asked.

"I see what you're doing. Very clever," said Vern. "Fine, I'll take you to Sacks. But I'm not driving the news van onto the property. If Thompson finds out I did this, my head will be on the chopping block."

April smiled at him. "Just think, Vern. For the rest of your life, you get to tell all your friends that you gave April O'Neil her first big break."

Vern grimaced. He had a feeling he was going to regret this.

CHAPTER 7

Eric Sacks's estate was a few miles north of New York City. It was an imposing compound nestled in the mountains. Though spring had warmed the City, snow and ice still clung to this area. April shivered in her thin yellow jacket as she approached the front gate.

She gave her name to the guard at the security booth, and eventually, the gate slid open. April followed the winding path to the front door. She was surprised when Eric Sacks opened the door himself. He greeted her warmly and invited her in.

"I'm sorry to barge in like this, Mr. Sacks," April apologized. "I was going to go through your press office, but I thought this should stay between us."

Sacks was intrigued. He led her farther into his sprawling home.

"I've been working on a story about the vigilantes protecting New York City, and I just had a big breakthrough. I think you and my father created the vigilantes."

Sacks stopped walking. April had his full attention. "That's impossible," he said. "We lost all our research in the fire, all our lab specimens, everything related to *Project Renaissance.*"

"You didn't lose everything," April told him. She took her cell phone out of her pocket. On the screen was the blurry photo of the four mutant turtles.

Sacks stared in surprise. His eyes widened in recognition. He'd spent the past fifteen years trying and failing to duplicate Dr. O'Neil's experiment. Now the results of that experiment were right before his eyes.

"The turtles are still alive," April said. "I've seen them."

"This is amazing," Sacks said. Then, putting a hand gently on her shoulder, he ushered her into a spacious room softly lit with candles. The walls were decorated with beautiful Japanese folding screens. The artwork on the screens illustrated a terrible time in the history of Japan.

"I was born on a military base in Japan. I learned many things there, such as Japanese history. These screens tell of a plague that ravaged the land. People died and chaos ruled. An evil warlord rose up and took control. A dark age of cruelty and brutality followed.

"I knew as a boy that I would do everything in my power to make sure that history like that never happened again. Luckily, I studied martial arts with a local sensei. He saw something in me, took me under his wing, and trained me in his *ashigaru dojo.* He believed that with enough focus and discipline, the mind was capable of amazing feats. People can do powerful and important things."

Sacks fixed April with an unblinking stare. "This was the purpose of my work with your father. We were looking for a cure to the diseases that caused those horrible events in Japan. Those turtles carry a secret in their blood that can save the world. By finding them, you've done a wonderful, world-changing thing. Your father would be very proud."

April held back tears as Sacks guided her to the front door of his mansion. He pressed an expensive, computerized business card into her hand.

"Please contact me if you need any help or you

think of anything I can do for you," Sacks said. "Together we will find those turtles and complete you father's work."

Sacks descended into the winding tunnels beneath his estate. They led to secret rooms and laboratories. He knew these passages by heart. In one dark corner he located a camouflaged panel and slid it open. He stepped into a hidden *dojo* and obediently addressed the powerful figure that knelt at the center of the room.

"Sensei, I have amazing news." Sacks's voice was hushed but excited. "The vigilantes that have caused us such trouble have been located—they are the turtles from my past experiment. In fact, it was the daughter of my old partner who found them. It's funny, really, that after all our searching, she should come to us with the information."

The dark master rose to his full height. "She told you where they were?"

Sacks shook his head. "Not exactly, but in time she will. I'm preparing a squad to capture them. Soon we shall have everything we need to proceed with our plan."

The master nodded. He did not impress easily, so this slight motion of approval was massive. Sacks was deeply pleased that he had satisfied his sensei, the teacher who had guided him since he was a boy in Japan.

"I have more good news for you," Sacks said as he led his teacher into an antechamber. "Your new armor is finished."

The metallic suit hung in the center of the room, shining cruelly in the glow of a single spotlight. It was a powerful mass of interlocking armored plates. The steely helmet was reminiscent of an ancient Shogun mask. The arms, gloves, and leg guards were adorned with multiple blades. They were long and curved, and would easily shred anything they touched.

"The robotics division of my company just completed it," Sacks whispered. "It bridges the gap between ancient armor and modern warfare."

Again, the teacher nodded. He was ready to lead his army, the Foot Clan, against the Turtles and to destroy New York City.

Shredder would be unstoppable.

"Tonight I will dine on turtle soup," he hissed.

CHAPTER 8

When Vern dropped April off at her apartment later that night, she was excited. She had the big story she had always wanted, and she was going to be able to complete her late father's work. But it all hinged on the Turtles, and she didn't know how to find them.

It was time to do what reporters did best—investigate.

April grabbed her laptop and pushed the power button. The screen came to life and exploded with color and light. Video-game music blared from the speakers, and an animated turtle moonwalked across the screen.

"Your computer has been hacked by the amazing Donatello!" a recorded voice announced. April watched the message, giggling slightly at its charm. It was an invitation to meet the Turtles on the roof where she'd first encountered them.

Well, she thought, *finding these guys wasn't so hard after all.*

An hour later, April waited on the roof. Around her the lights and sounds of New York City filled the night.

A breeze rustled past April. She became aware of someone behind her.

"Hi, lovely lady," Michelangelo said, stepping out of the shadows. "I hope you're ready for a date."

April was amazed by how quiet these giant turtles could be.

"It's not a date," said Leonardo.

"Yeah," Donatello said. "Plus, I'm the one who sent the invitation, so if anyone asked her out it was me." He turned to April. "Did you like the way I hacked your computer? I wrote the program myself. I'm used to faster computers, but I was able to work with yours."

Raphael pushed ahead of his brothers. "We don't have time for small talk. Let's just get her back to the lair. We're going to have to blindfold her."

Before April could respond, everything went black. It felt like a bag had been pulled over her head. A strong arm grabbed her waist, and the ground vanished beneath her feet. She was upside down and sailing through the air.

Her last thought before she passed out was *I'm falling from the building!*

When April woke up, she was inside the Turtles' underground lair. Michelangelo was eager to welcome her into the fold. He took her on a private tour of the lair.

"You guys live here? In the sewer?" she asked incredulously.

"Isn't it awesome?" Michelangelo replied.

April smiled awkwardly. It was hard for her to think of a sewer as home.

Michelangelo guided her through the tunnels. They walked from Donatello's impressive computer room to the spacious training room where the Turtles practiced their skills. The training area was stocked with all kinds of martial arts equipment. In the center of the room, Leonardo and Raphael faced off against robotic training dummies.

"We shouldn't have brought her here!"

Raphael shouted. He was arguing with his brother but venting his frustration on the dummy. "We should be out fighting the Foot Clan and hunting Shredder."

"Our first priority was April," Leonardo said reasonably. "Now that we're home, we can regroup, strategize, and pinpoint Shredder's location."

That idea wasn't good enough for Raphael. He didn't want to sit around and talk. He wanted to act. Raphael smashed his training dummy to pieces.

Leonardo let out a frustrated sigh. He was tired of Raphael always questioning his decisions. "Remember, this is what Splinter told us to do."

"If I were on my own, I'd be out getting stuff done," Raphael growled. He drew his *sai* and narrowed his eyes at his brother. Leonardo wasn't about to back down from a challenge. He drew his *katana* blade. The two Turtles lunged at each other.

At the sound of the commotion, Splinter hurried into the room. The wise master separated his fighting sons. Leonardo and Raphael backed away from each other under Splinter's disappointed gaze.

Splinter sat down with April. The four Turtles stood off to the side.

"When I last saw you, I could not properly thank you," Splinter said.

"Thank me?" April asked. "For what?"

"For saving our lives," Splinter answered. "You do not know it yet, but you are a warrior, Ms. O'Neil, destined to fight alongside us against the forces of darkness."

Splinter set down his walking stick and started telling a story. It was a story April thought she knew well. As she listened to his words, she remembered the terrible night her father died.

Dr. O'Neil had come to her in the middle of the night, waking her up. He told her they had to leave right away, that they were going on a trip. She smelled smoke, and the scream of fire alarms filled her ears. She knew the lab was on fire. She couldn't leave behind the test animals.

April ran through the smoke and made her way into the lab. She spotted the glass aquariums. The box turtles and lab rat were huddled into the corners of their cages.

Quickly, she opened the cages. She scooped all of the animals into her arms and ran for the exit. Outside, she set the turtles and the rat down next to a sewer drain. April turned to run back inside when suddenly the whole building exploded!

The blast was so strong it knocked April off her feet. She hit her head on the curb and passed out.

"Your father destroyed the lab because he learned that Sacks could not be trusted," Splinter said. "Sacks wanted to use their research for evil purposes. He didn't want to cure disease, he wanted to start a plague."

April was stunned. For so long she had recalled that story, remembered it, and repeated it to herself. But she had never known the *full* story.

Raphael's mouth dropped open. He was also stunned. He couldn't believe that this puny girl had saved *him*! Leonardo's elbow nudged him in the ribs. The four brothers bowed their heads and whispered thanks.

"We have more to be thankful for," Splinter said. "After you released us, we wandered the sewers as scared, defenseless animals. I didn't know how to care for these little turtles. But then I remembered the way your father cared for and protected you. And the way you cared for us in the lab. I knew I must protect the turtles as if there were my very own sons."

Splinter told April how the mutagen began to take effect. It did amazing things to them—made them bigger, stronger, and smarter than average animals. It also made him worried. They had become different, some might say freakish. He doubted the outside world would accept them.

"Remember how much fun we had as little turtles?" Michelangelo said. "Remember the games of Buck-Buck?"

Leonardo smiled and nodded. Buck-Buck was a simple game they used to play in a sewer tunnel that had a series of buckets hanging from an overhead pipe. On their own, the turtles couldn't reach any of the buckets; but they found that if they worked together, they could jump up and tap the buckets. One turtle would crouch and the others would run and spring off his shell. Soon they were able to perform intricate routines, jumping off each other and the walls,

banging the buckets again and again.

"Yes, Michelangelo," Splinter said. "It was a time of games. But they were important games— they were your first training. You see, I knew you had to learn to protect yourselves. I had discovered a book titled *The Art of the Ninja* and knew this was the key.

"For years I have protected my sons from the outside world," Splinter said. He was no longer looking at April. His gaze was far off. "Perhaps I have been overprotective, and I suppose it was inevitable that the world would find us."

April had been listening to Splinter's story and processing the information, making connections. She suddenly had a terrible realization.

"I don't think you should thank me anymore," she said with a worried whisper. "If Sacks cannot be trusted, then I've done a terrible thing. I've told him you exist. He knows all about you because of me! And he wouldn't have let me leave his estate unless he was planning on following me."

April became hot and sweaty with fear as she removed Sacks's business card from her pocket. She now knew it was a tracking device and that she had been used.

Splinter nodded. "The mutagen in our blood is still very valuable to him. He will not rest until he finds us. But we will be ready. We have stood together as a family and will fight as one, too."

Suddenly an alarm blared. An explosion shook the walls of the lair.

The battle would start sooner than they expected.

CHAPTER 9

The monitors in the training room flared to life. On the screens, dozens of Foot Soldiers marched toward the Turtles' lair.

KABOOM!

A massive explosion rocked the rooms. The force of the blast tore through the wall and knocked Raphael deep into the sewer tunnels. April was buried in rubble.

In the Turtles' bedroom, Leonardo, Donatello, and Michelangelo crawled out from under chunks of debris. A thick cloud of dust hung in the air.

They could barely see. They grabbed their weapons and set out to find Splinter and the others.

Splinter had been thrown into the dining area when the blast hit. The dark smoke from the explosion clouded his vision. The rodent closed his eyes. He knew there was something stronger than sight.

Splinter slipped into quiet meditation. After a moment, he felt an evil presence nearby. When he opened his eyes, Shredder was standing across from him.

"I've come to collect what's mine," Shredder said threateningly.

"We belong to no one," Splinter said defiantly.

Shredder's mechanized suit of armor stood out in contrast to Splinter's humble robes. Sharp blades winged from the shoulders and formed claws at the tips of his fingers. The blades whispered through the dense smoke as he stepped forward.

THEY FIGHT IN
SHADOW

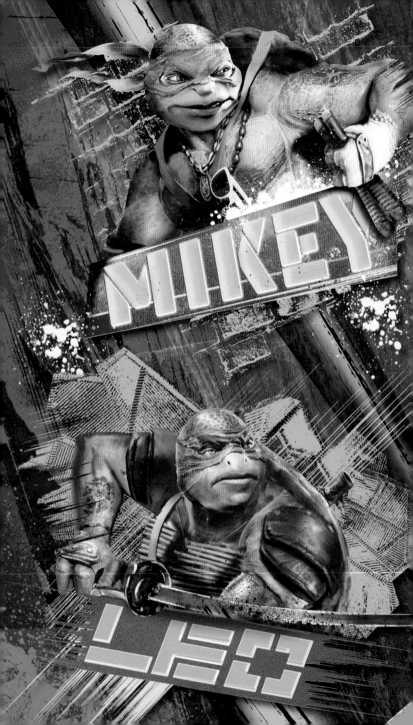

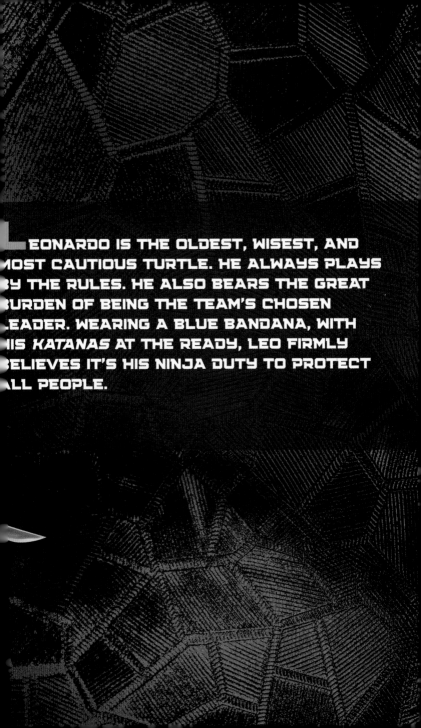

LEONARDO IS THE OLDEST, WISEST, AND MOST CAUTIOUS TURTLE. HE ALWAYS PLAYS BY THE RULES. HE ALSO BEARS THE GREAT BURDEN OF BEING THE TEAM'S CHOSEN LEADER. WEARING A BLUE BANDANA, WITH HIS *KATANAS* AT THE READY, LEO FIRMLY BELIEVES IT'S HIS NINJA DUTY TO PROTECT ALL PEOPLE.

THE TALLEST AND SMARTEST OF THE TURTLES, DONATELLO RELIES HEAVILY ON HIGH-TECH EQUIPMENT AND GEAR. HIS UNMATCHED INTELLIGENCE IS A HUGE ASSET TO HIS BROTHERS, WHO RELY ON HIM FOR ALL THEIR TECHNICAL NEEDS. SPORTING A PURPLE BANDANA, WITH A *BO* STAFF SLUNG ACROSS HIS BACK, DONNIE HAS BOTH BRAINS AND BRAWN.

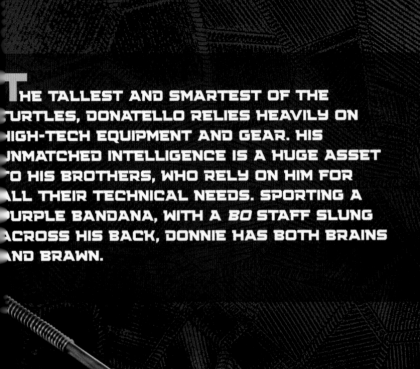

RAPHAEL

WITH HIS RED BANDANA, AND TWO *SAIS* IN HIS BELT, RAPHAEL IS THE BIGGEST BROTHER . . . AND HIS EGO IS EVEN BIGGER. NOT ONE TO HOLD BACK HIS TEMPER, RAPH IS AGGRESSIVE AND STRUGGLES WITH FOLLOWING ORDERS. HIS DEEP-SEATED FEAR OF BEING ALONE IS MASKED BY HIS FIERCE INDEPENDENCE AND TOUGH-GUY EXTERIOR.

MICHELANGELO

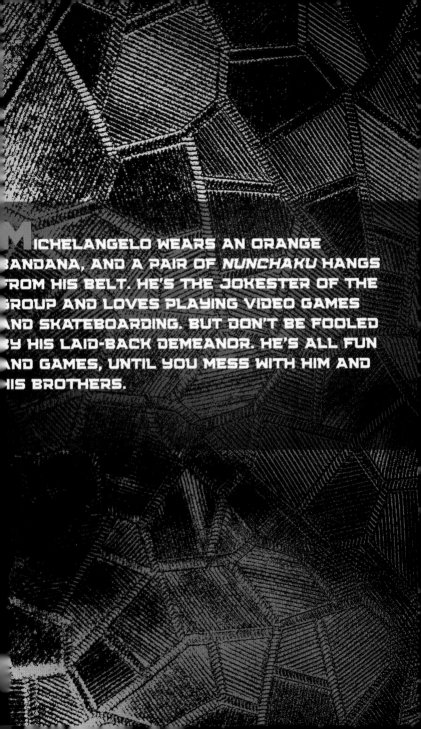

MICHELANGELO WEARS AN ORANGE BANDANA, AND A PAIR OF *NUNCHAKU* HANGS FROM HIS BELT. HE'S THE JOKESTER OF THE GROUP AND LOVES PLAYING VIDEO GAMES AND SKATEBOARDING. BUT DON'T BE FOOLED BY HIS LAID-BACK DEMEANOR. HE'S ALL FUN AND GAMES, UNTIL YOU MESS WITH HIM AND HIS BROTHERS.

ORIGINALLY AN EXPERIMENTAL LAB RAT, SPLINTER WAS INJECTED WITH DNA-INFUSED MUTAGEN THAT GAVE HIM SENTIENCE, THOUGHTS, AND A SOUL. AFTER AN UNFORTUNATE EVENT AT THE LAB, SPLINTER AND FOUR MUTANT BOX TURTLES FOUND THEMSELVES BUILDING THEIR NEW HOME IN THE SEWERS. SPLINTER TOOK ON A FATHERLY ROLE AND TRAINED THE TURTLES TO BECOME NINJA HEROES.

THE BONDS OF FAMILY ARE STRONGER THAN STEEL.

Splinter wielded his walking stick like a weapon. His tail swayed behind him, ready to strike.

Shredder was determined to capture the Turtles, and no one was going to stand in his way. He lunged forward, slicing through the air with his sharp claws.

Splinter dodged the strike. He wasn't as strong as Shredder in his power-driven suit, but he had the heart of a warrior. He was nimble and smart. Splinter maneuvered within Shredder's reach and delivered a series of quick blows.

Leonardo, Donatello, and Michelangelo ran into the dining room. They saw their sensei engaged in battle and rushed to help him. Security gates designed to protect the Turtles crashed into position, separating them from their teacher. Leo watched in horror through the bars. He struck the iron with his sword. Sparks flew, but it did nothing. Then dozens of Foot Soldiers stormed after the Turtles, driving them back from the battle between the two master warriors.

Splinter used his walking stick to block Shredder's blows. Shredder slashed with his claws and kicked wildly, challenging the rodent's agility. Splinter gave ground and backed through the dining area. He whipped his tail forward like a lash. He caught hold of Shredder's arm and pulled him off balance.

Shredder roared in frustration and renewed his attack. He pummeled Splinter with lightning-fast strikes, driving the rat into a corner.

"Never corner a rat," Splinter growled. He lifted his walking stick and drew a secret blade from inside it.

CHAPTER 10

The three Turtles battled wave upon wave of Foot Soldiers. Donatello let loose a sweeping blow of his *bo* staff that sent two soldiers tumbling. Then he dropped down and took out two more with a sweeping leg kick.

"Nice work, Donnie!" yelled Leo, who was fending off three soldiers with a dual *katana* attack.

Two soldiers jumped on Michelangelo. He grabbed them in his massive hands and smacked their heads together. They collapsed on the floor in a heap.

"Watch out!" Michelangelo bellowed. "I'm

a snapping turtle!" He cut through a crowd of soldiers with his *nunchucks*.

The Turtles were getting the upper hand . . . until a fresh squad of Foot Soldiers arrived with new weapons. They carried electrified stun prods. Donatello charged one of these soldiers and swung his staff. The soldier blocked it with his prod then jabbed. An electric bolt hit Donatello and sent him flying against a wall.

Another shocking blow hit Michelangelo. He dropped to his knees. He tried to stand, but a new bolt paralyzed him.

Splinter's sword moved quickly, deflecting the blades of Shredder's suit. He darted and ducked beneath the slashing claws, but it was clear Splinter was growing tired. Slowly, Shredder overpowered him, raining down a barrage of strikes.

"Sensei!" Leonardo screamed. He ran to the gate and rammed his shell against the bars, struggling to break them down.

"Go, my sons!" Splinter shouted. Bravely, he turned to face Shredder's blows. "Do not lay down your lives for an old rat like me. Live to fight another day!"

Shredder hammered the old sensei with another vicious attack. Splinter absorbed the devastating strikes, hoping to buy time for the Turtles to escape.

But Leonardo didn't turn and run. Instead, he froze and made a desperate decision.

"Shredder!" he yelled. "Will you let Splinter live if we surrender and come with you?"

Shredder paused. He looked at the Turtles and watched as Donatello and Michelangelo threw down their weapons. He then studied Splinter and decided the old teacher was not worth the effort it would take to destroy him. He turned his back on Splinter. The cruel metallic helmet nodded.

Leonardo closed his eyes and let his *katanas* fall to the stone floor. They echoed coldly through the silence of the ravaged lair.

Foot Soldiers swarmed Leonardo, Donatello, and Michelangelo. They bound the Turtles in chains. If one of the brothers tried to fight back, the attempt was weak and brought a zap from a prod.

"Ignore the pain," Leonardo moaned. "Pain is only in the mind."

The sting of electricity that followed these words made it hard for Leonardo to believe his own advice.

The Turtles were marched out of the lair and through the sewer. They emerged into a rainy, trash-strewn alleyway. The Foot Soldiers locked them in armored trucks. A signal was given. The engines roared to life, and the convoy pulled out.

Back in the lair, April stood slowly. She had been hit with rubble and ached all over, but she didn't think there was any serious damage. She wiped dust from her face and realized that Shredder was a few feet away. His back was to her, and she hadn't been seen. She carefully crouched behind a pile of debris and held her breath. She listened as a soldier made his report.

"The battle is over. We've captured three of the turtles and are transporting them up to the Sacks estate. The lab is waiting for them, ready to drain their blood."

"What about the fourth turtle?"

"He was destroyed in the blast. I saw it myself."

April bit her lip to stifle a cry. Could this all

be true? She didn't want to believe it. She felt sick and . . . responsible.

"Excellent," Shredder whispered. It all seemed so easy. He looked at the discarded weapons at his feet—a sword, a *bo* staff, a set of *nunchucks*. With a flick of his bladed metal boot, he sent them skittering down a flight of stairs, into a muddy puddle.

CHAPTER 11

The explosion in the lair had knocked Raphael deep into the sewers under a mountain of rubble. As soon as he dug free, he ran straight for Turtle headquarters. What he saw made his heart sink.

The lair was destroyed. Equipment was damaged, furniture was broken, and many of the walls had crumbled to dust. But that was nothing compared to finding Splinter. The sensei lay unconscious in the center of the training room. He was barely breathing.

"Sensei," Raphael whispered sadly. He sank to

the ground and pulled Splinter into his arms.

April emerged from the shadows. She was relieved to see that Raphael was alive. She wanted to hug him, but based on the brief time she'd known him, April was sure he wasn't the hugging type.

"What can I do?" she asked softly.

Raphael told April where to find a medical kit, and together they treated Splinter's wounds. Soon, he woke up.

"Raphael, you must rescue your brothers and stop Shredder," he whispered urgently.

"I know, Sensei. I'll get them back," Raphael promised.

"You cannot do it alone!" Splinter said. "If Shredder and the Foot are not stopped, a dark army will march across the face of this earth just as it did centuries ago. Only you stand in its way . . . both of you." Splinter looked from Raphael to April and then closed his eyes to rest.

"We have to get to the estate," April said. "I know someone who can drive."

"Good," Raphael grunted. He marched through the darkened lair, knocking over broken chairs and tables. After a few seconds, he found want he wanted.

"We'll need these," he said, collecting the swords, *bo* staff, and *nunchucks*. "Now let's go save my brothers."

Vern Fenwick stood next to a white news van, checking his hair in the side mirror. He had a fedora, but he wasn't sure if it looked good or not. He had received an urgent call from April and was pretty sure what she wanted. After all, he was a fine-looking guy, and they didn't work together anymore—why shouldn't they date?

"Come on, we have to get going," April said,

suddenly appearing next to him. "What's with the hat?"

"Hat? It's a friend's. I was trying it for a goof—unless you like it. Do you like it?"

April wasn't listening. She had climbed into the van's passenger seat and was glaring at him. Vern jumped behind the steering wheel, dropping the hat to the van's floor.

April quickly brought her former cameraman up to speed—the secret experiments, the Teenage Mutant Ninja Turtles, the fact that Sacks was working with Shredder to destroy New York City and possibly the world.

Vern stared at her. "C'mon, April, we're both adults. We don't need silly excuses to hang out. If you want to date, all you have to say is—"

Raphael leaned in between them from the back of the van.

"STOP TALKING AND GET THIS VAN

MOVING!" he roared. "WE HAVE TO SAVE MY BROTHERS!"

Vern was shocked. His first impulse was to ask what this creature was. But he realized that April had already told him. It was a mutant turtle. Next, he wondered how it had gotten into his van so quietly. *Well,* he told himself, *it's a ninja, and they're pretty stealthy.* Finally, he blurted out the only words he could think of: "You're a talking turtle!"

"And you're a talking nerd," Raphael growled back. "Now hit the gas!"

Vern gunned the engine, and the van peeled out.

In Sacks's laboratory, Leonardo, Donatello, and Michelangelo were growing weaker by the minute. They were suspended inside reinforced glass tanks. Thick chains held their arms and legs. Medical tubing wrapped around their bodies. The tubes wound out of the containment tanks and joined in a single hose that fed a large pulsing machine.

Sacks entered the room and got his first look at the result of his experiments. His jaw dropped and his eyes widened. "Wow! Look at you guys.

And to think, we were going to use rabbits instead of turtles. That would have been weird."

"Why are you doing this?" Leonardo asked weakly.

Sacks couldn't believe his ears. "Could you say that again?"

Leonardo asked again. His voice was already fainter.

"You're all part of my plan. We've created a deadly toxin, which we will bring to my building in the City. The spire at the top will act like a giant needle. We'll use it to release the disease."

To prove his power, Sacks motioned for his men to pull a Foot Soldier to the center of the room. While they held him, a breathing mask was strapped over the man's face. A hose connected the mask to a tank. A knob was turned. The sound of hissing gas could be heard. The man struggled and strained. His eyes bulged. After a few seconds, the man stopped moving and slid to the floor in a lifeless heap.

Sacks continued talking. "People will die. Chaos will ravage the City. This will have global implications. And who will be able to stop this disease? You will . . . well, your blood will. You see, the only remedy for our plague is hidden in your mutant blood. Thanks to you, only Sacks Enterprises will have the antidote. The governments of the world will send me a blank check. They will pay whatever price I demand to save the world."

Shredder swept into the room, his metal suit reflecting the overhead lights of the lab. "I find your devotion to money troubling. Don't you know that honor and power are all that matters?" He didn't look at his student. "How much longer will the process take?"

Sacks checked the collection machine. The

blood was dripping in slowly. There were multiple glass canisters. Only one was full.

"We have enough to get started," Sacks said. He flicked a switch and the blood-filled canister popped free with a pneumatic hiss. "We can fly this to the lab at headquarters and synthesize enough antidote to keep us safe when we release the toxin this afternoon."

Sacks called for his helicopter to be prepared. He and Shredder marched out of the lab.

The Channel 6 news van raced along the icy, winding road to Sacks's estate. The tires screeched with every turn. Vern's fists were white and sweaty on the steering wheel. He wanted to slow down and drive more carefully because they couldn't save anyone if they had an accident before they got to the estate. Also, he was responsible for any damages to the van. But each time he let up on the accelerator, the big turtle at this shoulder leaned forward and breathed hot breath on his neck.

Finally, the estate came into view. But there was one problem.

"April, the front gate is locked!" Vern screamed. "What'll we do?"

"Drive faster," Raphael grunted.

Vern stepped on the gas and closed his eyes.

CRASH!

The van burst through the gate, sending shreds of wood and metal flying. It raced into a courtyard and skidded to a halt. Vern jumped out and surveyed the damage.

"My poor van!" he moaned. The headlights were smashed, the fender twisted. The van rocked as Raphael burst out the back, wrenching one door from its hinges. "Hey!" Vern yelled. "Those doors open, you know. You don't have to smash everything!"

Before Vern could continue his rant, Foot Soldiers stormed the yard. Raphael plowed into them, his *sais* flashing. His fists sent three soldiers flying. A thunderous kick toppled two more.

"Follow me!" Raphael yelled over his shoulder. They raced into the estate.

Raphael was the first to reach the top of the stairs. He burst through the door into Sacks's laboratory. Leonardo, Donatello, and Michelangelo were almost completely drained of blood. Raphael rushed toward the glass cages.

"The fourth cage is for you," Shredder said menacingly. He dove out of the shadows and tackled Raphael. Shredder was the first to rise in his armored samurai suit. He kicked Raphael and pounded him with a series of powerful strikes, knocking him into the next room.

Raphael rolled to his feet and drew his *sais*. The sound of metal on metal rang out as he used his *sais* to deflect Shredder's blows. He spun quickly, dodging the sharp claws of the samurai suit.

April and Vern rushed into the laboratory and ran to the glass cages. April heard the fight coming from next door. With Shredder preoccupied, she was free to focus on saving the other Turtles. But what should she do? The glass containers and monitors were a mass of lights, tubes, and wires. She tapped Donatello's cage gently.

"Can you hear me? What do I do?" she asked.

Donatello was almost too weak to speak. "Adrenaline," he said, motioning toward a monitor with his weary nod.

"Which button is it?" April asked urgently.

Donatello didn't answer. His eyes slipped closed. April banged against his cage anxiously. "Come on, Donnie! I need your help."

April studied the touch screen. She shuffled through a menu and found an icon labeled "adrenaline." She touched it.

The machine gurgled to a stop. The pumps reversed, sending the Turtles' blood back into their bodies. It also provided a much needed dose of energy-restoring hormones.

Instantly, the Turtles' eyes flew open. Donatello, Michelangelo, and Leonardo jumped to their feet. They broke the chains and ripped the tubes out of their arms. They smashed through the glass cages.

"Wow! I feel great," Michelangelo exclaimed. "Like really great!" He flexed his arm muscles and admired them.

"I know!" Donatello agreed. "I've got loads of

energy. We should clean something. Who wants to go to the lair and clean up my lab?"

"Maybe I gave them too much adrenaline," April said to Vern.

Leo turned to April and Vern, and told them about Sacks, the toxin, and the helicopter.

"We have to stop them," April said.

"First we have to save Raphael," Leonardo replied.

Next door, Shredder backed Raphael into a corner. The samurai suit gave him added strength and protected him from Raphael's blows. Shredder was relentless, landing punch after punch. He hit Raphael repeatedly until he drove the turtle to the ground.

Raphael struggled to rise, but Shredder was too fast for him. He stomped down hard on the turtle's back, cracking his shell!

Shredder removed his foot. "I could destroy you, but without your brothers, you are no longer a threat. Plus, we will need your blood. We need you alive . . . for now."

Shredder turned and left the room.

Raphael's friends and brothers ran to his side. "How are you?" Leonardo asked.

"My shell has felt better," Raphael groaned.

Donnie pulled a first aid kit from his belt and went to work on Raphael's wound.

"Thanks, Donnie," Raphael said. "I have something for you, too." He handed Donatello his *bo* staff. He also gave Leonardo his *katanas* and Michelangelo his *nunchucks*.

The Teenage Mutant Ninja Turtles stood together, armed and ready for battle. They were a lean, green fighting machine.

CHAPTER 13

The Turtles led April and Vern out of the secret compound. They ran stealthily down its long, twisting corridors. One by one they picked off the Foot Soldiers patrolling the halls. The Turtles smashed them into walls and hurled them aside as if they weighed nothing at all. After a few more tunnels and battles, they reached the door to the courtyard.

"We'll just hop in the van and be back in New York in no time," Leonardo said. "Everybody ready?" He opened the door carefully.

The news van was just where they had left it. Unfortunately, it was surrounded by two dozen Foot Soldiers. They stood at attention, weapons ready.

"This isn't going to be as easy as I hoped," Leonardo said.

"Fine by me," Raphael said, smashing his fist into his open hand. "Let's do this."

The Turtles went to work dispatching black-clad villains left and right. Powerful blows and kicks sent the soldiers flying. One jumped up with a gun. Leo quickly grabbed April and spun around. The bullet glanced off his shell.

"Hey!" Leonardo exclaimed. "Our shells our bulletproof!"

A group of soldiers produced a portable rocket launcher. They sighted Michelangelo and fired. A massive burst of flame and smoke leaped across the courtyard. Michelangelo felt the heat and sprang into the air. A spectacular backflip carried him over the missile, which exploded into a far wall.

"Awesome jump!" Donatello yelled.

Michelangelo did a short moonwalk. "What can I say? I've got mad moves."

At last they reached the van. April jumped into the passenger seat. Vern slammed the accelerator to the floor. The Turtles jumped in the back.

Donnie fired up a laptop. His fingers flew across the keys. Maps flashed across the screen.

"Just as I thought, twelve miles from here there's a sewer entry that leads to the City," Donnie announced. "If we can get there, we're home free!"

The van barreled across the courtyard. A large, black Humvee roared out of the shadows, blocking the only exit. A soldier was perched on top of the vehicle manning a dangerous machine gun. He fired and blew out one of the van's tires.

Vern struggled for control, but there was nothing he could do. The van skidded across the courtyard and ran into a tractor-trailer parked near the wall.

"Time to trade up," Michelangelo said, eyeing the eighteen-wheeler.

Vern and April hopped out of the news van and climbed up into the cab of the semi.

"There must be a way to hotwire this," Vern said as he fumbled with some wires hanging from the dashboard.

April swatted the overhead visor. A set of keys tumbled down.

"You could also use those," April said.

"Thanks," Vern said. He turned the ignition and the engine roared to life.

Michelangelo bounced up onto the roof of the truck. He spotted a fleet of SUVs pulling up alongside the Humvee.

"We've got company coming," he called down to his brothers.

Leonardo, Donatello, and Raphael climbed into the back of the truck. Michelangelo thumped the roof to signal Vern. He threw the eighteen-wheeler into gear and rumbled across the courtyard.

Soon, the big rig was barreling down the snowy mountain roads outside the estate with the Foot in pursuit. Shredder's forces drove heavily armored SUVs. They were fast and surprisingly agile.

One truck peeled left and tried to pull alongside the giant semi. Vern caught sight of it in the side-view mirror and nudged the steering wheel. The massive semi swerved, knocking the truck into the guard rail. A wave of sparks shot up as it almost rolled into an icy ravine. The driver regained control and fell back behind the eighteen-wheeler.

One Foot Soldier manned a roof-mounted weapon and opened fire. Shots rang off the rig and whizzed past the cab.

Michelangelo clung to the roof of the semi in order to avoid being thrown. Leonardo wasn't as lucky. He tumbled off the back of the truck, crashing hard into the snowy slope. But the Turtles' leader recovered quickly. He slid downhill on his back using his shell as a sled.

One of the SUVs roared after Leonardo. A soldier leaned out of the side of the speeding vehicle. He fired an electrified cable through the air. The cable wrapped around Leonardo's arm and sent a jolt of electricity coursing through his body.

Raphael and Donatello watched from the back of the semi. They had to help their brother!

"Allow me," Donatello said. He took a running leap from the back of the truck.

Donatello landed next to Leonardo and slid down the hill beside him. He pulled a small gadget from his belt and cut the electrified bolo from his brother's arm. The cable whipped backward and slammed into the soldier who fired it.

"I hate being left out of all the fun!" Michelangelo announced. He dove off the roof of the truck yelling, "CANNONBALL!"

He tucked his head and limbs inside his shell and hurtled through the air, crashing through the windshield of an enemy SUV. Michelangelo popped out of his shell in the front seat. He rammed the Foot Soldiers' heads together and swiftly bailed from the vehicle. The SUV slid across the icy road and smashed into a snow drift.

Back in the semi, Vern spotted trouble on the horizon. The huge tractor-trailer was headed directly for a cliff! Vern down-shifted and pumped the breaks, but the truck was moving too fast. The semi fishtailed. The entire rear of the eighteen-wheeler slid violently out of control.

Leonardo and Donatello saw the truck go into a skid. "We have to straighten it out!" Leonardo said. They tucked themselves into their shells and tobogganed down the slope beside the semi. Donatello reached out and grabbed onto the vehicle's undercarriage. He pulled himself and his brother beneath the truck.

Moments later, Michelangelo and Raphael joined them. The four Turtles used their shells as rudders against the ground. They guided the truck back into position. But when Michelangelo looked up, he saw the cliff's edge dead ahead.

"Dudes! End of the line!" he shouted to his brothers.

"Blue Forty-Two!" Leonardo called like the captain of a football team. The other Turtles nodded. They understood the play.

Raphael grabbed hold of Leonardo's arm and slung him out from beneath the truck. At the same time, Michelangelo rolled out from under the vehicle. He launched himself into the air and landed on Leonardo's belly, using his brother as a snowboard.

Michelangelo surfed beside the cab of the eighteen-wheeler. He motioned for April and Vern to jump to safety.

A blast sounded somewhere behind them. Michelangelo looked back in time to see a rocket sizzling toward him.

"Incoming!" he yelled and ducked. The fireball bounced off the side of the semi's cab and spiraled into the woods. The door of the cab flew open, and April was knocked loose. She grabbed the seat belt and hung on for dear life.

Leonardo bucked Michelangelo free and jumped into the cab to protect April. Meanwhile,

Raphael and Donatello had a plan of their own beneath the truck.

"Batter up!" Raphael shouted.

Donatello extended his *bo* staff and used it to sling Raphael into the Foot Clan's vehicle. It tumbled over and smashed into a nearby tree.

Donatello dropped free of the semi just as its front wheels slid off the cliff. The eighteen-wheeler plunged over the edge.

"No!" Michelangelo screamed. "We lost them! We'll never see Leo, April, and that other guy again!"

Donatello, Michelangelo, and Raphael raced toward the cliff. There was no sign of Leonardo, April, or Vern. The brothers peered over the edge and were relieved by what they saw. Leonardo's sword was stuck into the side of the cliff. He hung one-handed from the hilt. In his other hand hung April and Vern.

Leonardo smiled up at his brothers as if to say: all in a day's work. He helped April and Vern climb up to solid ground.

"Where do we go from here?" Raphael asked.

Donatello looked around, and then pointed to a pile of snow. "If my calculations are correct, we're going right there."

He brushed aside the snow and revealed a manhole cover emblazed with the letters *NYC*.

CHAPTER 14

The Sacks Tower was one of the tallest buildings in New York City. Its pointed iron spire extended high into the clouds. The building was a shining beacon of hope for the people of New York. But they had no idea of the danger brewing inside.

On the thirty-sixth floor was a state-of-the-art laboratory. Sacks had spent years here conducting experiments, failing time and again. All those years of effort would pay off today.

"We have just enough toxin to poison ten

square blocks of the City," Sacks said. "It's a start. Soon we'll have more."

He pressed a button and activated a machine. He slipped the canister of turtle blood into a chamber and went to work.

"The first dose of antidote is almost ready, Master Shredder," he said, watching the swirling blood and chemicals turn into bubbling green mutagen.

"Excellent," Shredder said. "Today is a great day. For too long I have lived in the shadows. It is finally my time to take the power that is rightfully mine and punish those who have denied me my honor."

It's also time to make a load of money, Sacks thought. But he knew better than to say that out loud again.

Shredder went to the spire to release the toxin.

The Turtles, April, and Vern pushed aside a manhole cover and climbed into the basement of Sacks Enterprises. It was time to split up: Vern and April would search for Sacks and his lab; the Turtles would disable the spire.

"When you find the mutagen," Leonardo said, "make sure you save it. We might need to help a lot of people with it."

"It could also help Splinter," Donatello added.

"Are you sure you'll be okay?" Raphael asked.

April nodded. "I've taken a few kickboxing lessons, and I think I've picked up a few things from you guys."

The team went their separate ways.

The Turtles crowded into an elevator and pushed the top button. The car started to rise through the interior of the building. The four brothers didn't say a word.

Raphael anxiously tapped his *sais* together. *Clink-clink-clink.*

Leonardo picked up on the rhythm with his *katanas. Zip-zip, zip-zip-zip, zip.*

Michelangelo and Donatello laid down beats on top of the sound. By the time they reached the top floor, they had a full rap going.

A bell rang and the elevator doors opened onto a room filled with Foot Soldiers. The Turtles stopped the music. It was time for battle.

They charged with weapons drawn.

Many floors below the Turtles' raging battle, April and Vern crept quietly into the laboratory. Sacks was alone, overseeing his pulsing machine. He spoke without turning to look at them.

"History repeats itself," he said with a chuckle. "Your father snuck into my lab and tried to stop

my experiments. Now it seems to be your turn."

He spun and fired a gun. The bullet ricocheted off a desk.

Vern and April dropped to the floor. Vern kept crawling forward, searching the floor.

"What are you doing?" April said frantically.

"Looking for a plug," Vern answered. He swept his hands through a nest of wires beneath a control panel. He couldn't make heads or tails of the circuitry.

"We don't have time for this!" April yelled. She jumped and grabbed a chair. She heaved it into a control panel. Sparks flew into the air.

"Stop!" Sacks cried, firing another bullet. "Step away from my machine!"

"It's not your machine!" April said defiantly. "This is my father's work, and I won't let you use it for evil."

"Let me?" Sacks laughed. "I stopped your

father, and I will stop you. It just might take a few more bullets."

Sacks tightened his grip on the weapon. His finger tensed on the trigger.

April didn't back down. "You don't have the guts to shoot me."

Sacks fired the gun! Vern pushed April out of the way, forcing her to the ground. Unfortunately, the bullet grazed him in the shoulder. April rolled forward, and took Sacks down with a spinning kick. The scientist tumbled, dropping the gun.

April caught it and raised it over her head. She squeezed a shot into the fire alarm overhead. Sirens wailed and fire-extinguishing foam sprayed from nozzles in the ceiling.

Sacks glared at her. She leveled the gun at him. He turned and ran.

April let out a relieved gasp and crawled to Vern's side. The cameraman was hurt, but his injuries weren't life-threatening. "I thought he didn't have the guts to shoot you," Vern said with a grimace.

"He didn't shoot me," April pointed out. She helped Vern to a sitting position and quickly bandaged his shoulder.

Unexpectedly, April's cell phone buzzed. She pulled it out of her pocket and looked at the screen. There was a text from Donatello. It read: *S.O.S.*

Vern saw the message and pushed April toward the door. "Go. They need you. I'll be fine," he said.

"What am I supposed to do?" April asked worriedly. She was scared. She wanted to help the Turtles, but she didn't know how. "You saw that armored suit. Shredder's practically invincible!"

At a loss, April scanned the room. Her eyes came to rest on a vial of glowing, green liquid. With the mutagen machine destroyed, this was the only vial of antidote. April grabbed the mutagen and raced toward the roof.

CHAPTER 15

On the roof of the Sacks building, Shredder stood at the base of the towering spire, typing codes into a computer. A countdown started on the screen. In five minutes the deadly toxin would be released into the blustery morning sky. The people on the streets below would never know what hit them.

The four Turtles stepped onto the roof and prepared for their greatest fight ever. Their

opponent turned to face them. The sun reflecting from his armor and blades was nearly blinding.

"Mikey, do you remember that word you used to say all the time?" Leonardo asked. "The one I told you never to say again?"

"Sure do," Michelangelo replied.

"Do you think you have one more in the tank?"

Michelangelo nodded, smiled, and yelled, "COWABUNGA!"

Raphael led the charge. He ducked Shredder's strikes and lashed out with his *sais*. The sharp metal prongs clashed against Shredder's armor, driving him back a few steps.

Leonardo, Donatello, and Michelangelo jumped out to help Raphael. They closed ranks around their brother, deflecting Shredder's blows. Shredder advanced, kicking and slashing with his claws. The mechanized samurai suit made him almost invincible.

"Donnie, we'll draw Shredder away from the spire," Leonardo said. "You get to the computer and see if you can stop that countdown."

Donatello sprang into action and went wide, using a line of giant ventilation ducts as cover. Leonardo went straight at Shredder. He led with his swords for protection and followed with a roundhouse kick. It barely moved the dark master.

Michelangelo was next. He whirled his *nunchucks* in front of him with lightning speed. The powerful rods struck Shredder repeatedly. They did almost no damage.

But the plan was working. Donatello had reached the computer and was typing furiously.

Raphael and Shredder tangled. *Sais* met blades and threw sparks. Kicks were blocked, punches rebuffed. The robotic warrior tossed Raphael back against a safety railing. It barely held.

The Turtles regrouped and surrounded Donatello.

"How are you doing?" Leonardo asked.

"It's a complex program but not impossible to crack," Donatello said. "They're using a dual-level security algorithm with a random number—"

"In English, Donnie!"

"About one more minute should do it."

Raphael glanced at the countdown. The clock hit sixty seconds, and the numbers just kept melting away. "That's about all the time you have!"

(58 . . . 57 . . . 56 . . . 55 . . .)

Shredder marched toward the Turtles. Leonardo thought he could feel each step shaking the roof. They would need a new plan in order to defeat Shredder.

(42 . . . 41 . . . 40 . . .)

Leonardo had an idea. It seemed crazy, but it might be their only hope.

"Who's up for a quick game of Buck-Buck?" he asked.

Raphael and Michelangelo looked at their

brother like he'd been hit in the head one too many times, but then they understood.

(31 . . . 30 . . . 29 . . .)

"I'll go first!" Michelangelo shouted with glee. He charged at Shredder, but just before he reached him, he dropped to the ground. Raphael was right behind him. He sprang off his brother's shell. His mighty kick connected with Shredder's helmet.

The metallic warrior was momentarily stunned. He stepped back, and before he could react, Raphael had dropped into a ball at his feet. Leonardo used his brother as a springboard and sent rapid punches into Shredder's chest.

(15 . . . 14 . . . 13 . . .)

The Turtles kept rolling this way, each taking turns leaping and striking. They attacked with multiple blows from all sides. Instead of a collection of individual brawlers, they had become a single, fluid battle machine. Shredder could not respond.

(6 . . . 5 . . . 4 . . .)

"Did it!" Donatello yelled. The frozen clock displayed one second. He jumped up and used his *bo* staff to pole vault into the action alongside his brothers.

Shredder wasn't defeated yet. With a terrible roar, he threw Raphael and Michelangelo across the roof. Then he stretched out his arms and released a dozen missile-driven daggers. Leonardo ducked, and the blades sliced the air over his head.

They struck the spire, shaking it. Shredder fired another barrage of daggers. These shook the tower again—and cut into its supports.

He was no longer interested in the Turtles. He wanted to knock over the tower.

More blades sliced into it.

The metal groaned and the tall spire leaned precariously. One more hit and the spire would collapse, falling onto the hundreds of people in Times Square!

CHAPTER 16

The Turtles ran to support the tower. Each brother grasped a leg and strained to keep the spire standing. The weight was unbelievable. The rivets creaked and whined.

"What'll we do if this falls?" Michelangelo asked. "What's Plan B?"

"There is no Plan B," Leonardo grunted. He looked up and saw the tank of toxin nestled inside the framework of the spire. "Failure is not an option!"

"Why do you try to postpone the inevitable?"

Shredder roared triumphantly. "The Foot will stomp out the world!"

"Not if we stomp you first!" April shouted, running onto the roof.

Shredder turned his back on the Turtles and stalked slowly toward April.

"Your army's not coming! We destroyed the machine," April said fiercely. She held the vial of mutagen up for Shredder to see. "This is all that's left of the mutagen!"

Enraged, Shredder lunged at April. She sprinted quickly to the edge of the roof and held the vial out over the street below. "Take another step and I'll drop it," she warned him.

"What do you think you're doing?" Shredder asked, his voice dripping with menace.

"Finishing what my father started," she answered boldly. She locked eyes with Shredder, challenging him.

Raphael's muscles strained. He knew he couldn't hold the tower up much longer—and if he was tired, his brothers must be, too? He looked around the roof, searching for a solution. His eyes came to rest on a neighboring building.

Donatello followed his brother's gaze. He ran a quick mental simulation and nodded to Raphael. The crazy idea might just work.

They lined up their shells against the spire's beams and pushed.

"I don't like this, Donnie," Leonardo whispered, looking down at Times Square. "There are civilians everywhere. What about collateral damage?"

"The plan is sound," Donatello replied. "I triple-checked my calculations, and have my calculations ever let you guys down?"

The other Turtles shook their heads. Donatello was always right when it came to math. They pushed against the beams, weakening the spire.

April saw the spire begin to crumble. She knew she had to keep Shredder distracted a little longer. She waved the mutagen precariously over the edge of the roof.

"Your father worked his whole life for that. It was his greatest creation," Shredder snarled, struggling to convince her.

"You don't know a thing about my father!" April shouted.

The spire's steel beams finally snapped, and the huge metal structure fell through the air!

CHAPTER 17

Both Shredder and April stood directly in the path of the falling spire. In his robo-powered suit, Shredder could easily have escaped, but the mutagen was more important to him.

He launched himself at April.

They grappled.

The spire crashed down, dragging both of them over the edge of the roof.

The top of the spire swung out over Times Square and smashed into the roof of the skyscraper next door. Fortunately, the second building

stopped the spire from falling. The steel structure hung between the two buildings like a bridge.

The Turtles rushed to the edge of the roof, desperate to find April. They were shocked to see her hanging from the middle of the spire. Shredder's armored suit had protected both of them from the crash. Now April dangled one-handed from the spire bridge. She clutched the vial of mutagen in her other hand.

To make matters worse, Shredder also hung from the bridge. He swung toward April, determined to grab the mutagen. April was terrified. Her hands were sweating. She struggled to maintain her grip on the spire, but she ran out of strength.

April screamed and squeezed her eyes shut as her hand slipped free. Luckily, Raphael arrived just in time. He grabbed April by the wrist and whisked her out of the air. She opened her eyes to see that the Turtles had formed a chain along the spire, stretching out to meet her.

She also noticed that the metal Shredder was gripping was twisting. It couldn't withstand the tremendous weight of his armor. He reached for a more secure bar.

April had an idea. "Swing me!" she yelled to Raphael. He grabbed her hand tightly and gave a mighty heave. She sailed through the air, leading with her feet.

The kick hit Shredder in the chest. On solid ground he probably wouldn't have felt it. But in his unsteady position, it was enough to send him tumbling through the air, falling hundreds of feet to the ground.

Raphael hoisted April and the mutagen up to the spire. She grabbed on, took a deep breath, and felt the steel structure shudder. The giant spire groaned, and the temporary bridge between the two buildings started to roll toward the edge of both roofs.

Raphael glared at Donatello. "I thought you triple-checked the calculations!"

"I didn't account for the weight of a girl, a man in a titanium suit, and four giant turtles! Nobody's perfect!" Donatello replied, exasperated.

The Turtles tried to shift their weight, but it was no use. The movement only increased the spire's momentum. It rolled along the rooftops and careened over the edge! Leonardo, Donatello, Raphael, and Michelangelo dug their weapons into the sides of the building. They struggled to stop the spire's descent, but it spiraled down to the street below.

"Anybody have any last words?" Leonardo asked.

"I'm sorry I'm always so hard on you guys," Raphael yelled. "You're my brothers and I love you.

If I get too mean, it's because I don't think I deserve you and can never do enough to help you!"

SCREECH!

The spire came to a halt. When the dust cleared, April and the Turtles saw that the twisted wreckage had scraped to a stop against another building. They were all hanging about three inches above the ground.

"Talk about close calls," Michelangelo said, dropping to the sidewalk.

"What were you saying about not being good enough for us?" Leonardo asked Raphael. April wasn't sure if turtles could blush, but she thought the big guy's cheeks started to match his red bandana.

"Cowabunga!" Raphael said with a smile.

Leonardo flipped open a sewer cover. "We've got to get this mutagen to Splinter. It should do him a lot of good."

The Turtles said goodbye and vanished into

the tunnels beneath the City. April quietly slipped away, too. She wanted to check on Vern. And she wanted to report her first big story.

The Turtles returned to the remains of their lair and found Splinter still lying in the center of the training room. His eyelids fluttered weakly as they approached. He could barely speak. Donnie knew there was no time to waste. He crouched and administered a dose of the mutagen.

The color quickly returned to the sensei's cheeks and his eyes were suddenly bright. His tail was alert. He sat up with some difficulty as his sons gathered around.

Leonardo spoke softly. "We stopped the Foot Clan for now, Master, but you were right, we weren't ready."

"No, Leonardo, it was I who was not ready."

The strength had returned to Splinter's voice. "I wasn't prepared to let you journey to the outside world, to trust you. Now I see you were ready and that all along your greatest strength was your belief in each other."

Raphael gave Splinter a helpful, steadying hand as he slowly climbed to his feet. Michelangelo recovered Splinter's staff for him. The Turtles stood with their father and teacher and surveyed the devastated lair.

"It is time to rebuild," Splinter said.

Police and ambulances raced to Times Square. Crowds gathered around the destruction. They pointed and gasped and posed for selfies in front of the wreckage. Gradually the police were able to force back the crowds.

In all the confusion there was one pile of

rubble that went unnoticed. It surrounded a very deep crater. At the bottom there was a lot of shattered metal.

No one noticed the shiny metal glove.

The serrated fingers made a defiant fist.

CHAPTER 18

A few days later, as the sun set over the Hudson River, April rode her bike through the streets of New York. The City that had come so close to destruction seemed to be back to normal. It was almost like the events of the last few days had never happened.

But April knew they had happened. And she knew everything wasn't back to normal. The police had picked up Sacks, but Shredder was still missing.

Knowing he was out there was disturbing. But she also knew that there were forces for good on the lookout, ready to step in and help.

She rode her bike through the Lower East Side and stopped beneath a darkened overpass along the East River. The lights of Brooklyn glowed in the distance.

"How ya doin', Red?" It was Vern. His shoulder was bandaged and his arm was in a sling, but he was smiling. "Do you like the Fenwickmobile?" He nodded toward a pristine white car behind him.

"It's very cool."

"Well, it's not mine yet. Channel 6 helped me buy it, but it's mine to pay off. In a few months it will be the new Fenwickmobile." He patted the hood gently. "It was pretty understanding of them after what I did to the van."

"They couldn't have been too mad after the story you brought them," April said.

"*We* brought them," Vern corrected her. "It looks like we'll be working together again. That is, if the station's star reporter will have me."

"I wouldn't want another cameraman," April said.

Vern blushed. "I was thinking, even though we are a professional team again, it doesn't mean we can't go out to dinner. I know you aren't much for fancy restaurants, but there's a place that—"

Vern was interrupted by a passing van. It crawled slowly past and stopped. Heavy music thumped from inside. The vehicle looked like it was patched together from a dozen other cars and trucks. The side door slid open, and Michelangelo popped out.

"What's up, pretty lady, and, um, other guy?" he asked. "How are you all doing?"

Raphael popped from behind him. Leonardo and Donatello leaned out of either side of the front of the van.

"Do you like our new van?" Leonardo asked.

"We call it the *Shellraiser*," Raphael said. "Donnie built it."

"Ah, it's nothing," Donnie said with a shrug. "Though it is fully armored and has state-of-the-art surveillance and tracking systems."

"And a kickin' sound system, as you can hear," Michelangelo added. Then, reaching inside the van, he announced, "I have a special song I want to sing to you right now."

But the song didn't change. In fact, the music stopped and an improvised rocket launcher sprang up through the sunroof.

"Oops," Michelangelo said with a chuckle. "I must have pushed the wrong button. Maybe it's this one—"

The missile fired from the launcher. It sailed across the street and totaled the soon-to-be Fenwickmobile.

Vern was stunned. "My car" was all he was able to whisper again and again. "My new car."

Michelangelo covered his mouth. "Oops. My bad."

Police sirens sounded in the distance. They quickly grew louder.

"Sorry, dude," Leonardo said. "We'd love to hang around and help you with your car, but we've got to get out of here. Don't worry, you'll be seeing us again."

The door slammed shut and the windows were rolled up. The ramshackle *Shellraiser* sped away into the night. Vern and April decided it was best to leave, too.

Later, as April biked home, she rolled over a manhole cover in the street. It made her smile. She knew that heroes came in all shapes and sizes. They weren't necessarily wealthy billionaires. They weren't always square-jawed comic book heroes with flowing capes and movie star good looks.

Heroes are just like you and me, April thought. *Or they can be real-life superheroes who save a city. Sometimes heroes come in a half shell.*